Dedicated to Teak Dyer

A Book by Rod Dyer Group . . . .

Design: Steve Twigger, Rod Dyer Group, Inc.

Art Direction: Rod Dyer

Copyright © 1990 by Rod Dyer Group, Inc.
All Rights Reserved. Printed in Hong Kong.
Library of Congress Cataloging in Publication Data.

Dyer, Rod and Passwaters, Tiffany
Who likes rain? by Rod Dyer and Tiffany Passwaters:
illustrations by Paul Leith
p.   ca.
Summary: Rhymed text and illustrations introduce a
variety of animals found on a farm.
ISBN 0-87701-697-6
(1. Domestic animals–Fiction. 2. Farm life–Fiction.
3. Stories in rhyme.)
I. Leith, Paul, ill. II. Title.   89-25443
PZ8.3.P2723Far 1989   CIP
(E)–dc20   AC

Distributed in Canada by Raincoast Books
112 East Third Avenue, Vancouver, B.C. V5T 1C8

10 9 8 7 6 5 4 3 2 1

Chronicle Books,
275 Fifth Street
San Francisco, California 94103

Who likes rain?

by Rod Dyer and Tiffany Passwaters

Chronicle Books | San Francisco

Let's go to the farm

for a day full of fun.

But what will we do

if there's rain and no sun?

Hello, **rooster**,

on the weather vane.

Is it going to be windy?

Do you think it will rain?

"I hope there's
no rain,"
said the **sheep**
in a fret.

"I can't make
warm sweaters
if my wool
is all wet!"

"Rain helps the grass grow,"

said the **cow** with a wink.

"I need to eat lots

to make the milk that you drink."

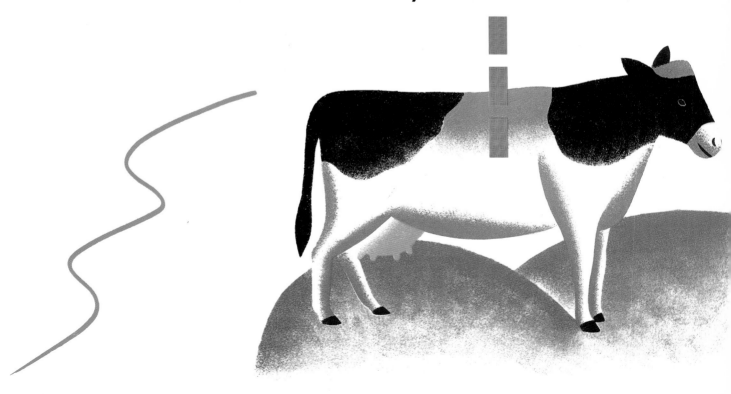

"I hope that it rains", said the **duck** with a quack.

"I love to swim in the water and feel the drops on my back!"

"Neigh," said the **horse** with a mouth full of hay.
"I hope there's no rain so you can ride me today."

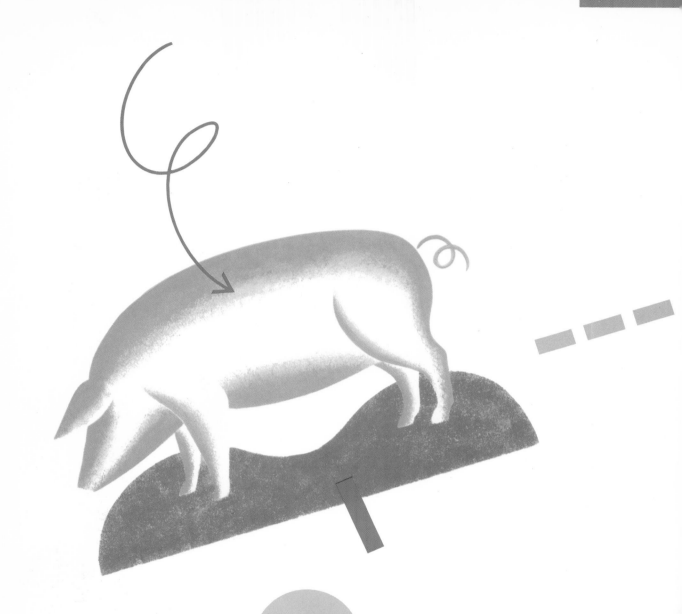

"Oink, oink," said the pig as he fell with a thud.
"I love when it rains, and I can play in the mud!"

"Whoooo,"
hooted the owl
with a turn of
his head.
"Who
likes rain?
It's the
wetness
I dread."

"I do, I do," croaked the **toad** with a jump.

"When it rains I have parties in the old tree stump."

"Caw,
caw,"
cried the crow
as she guarded
her nest.

"The rain scares
my babies,
and then
they can't rest."

"Well, hello," said the **rabbit**
with a hippity-hop.
"I don't mind if it rains
because I know
it will stop."

"Hush," said the fox,

sneaking around.

"I don't mind the rain

as long as there's food to be found!"

"Squeak!"

peeped the mouse
as he scurried
out of sight.
"I'm afraid of
the rain,

and the thunder gives
me a fright."

"Woof,"

barked the **dog**.
"Please rain
another day.
My friend's come
to visit and
we want
to play!"

"Honk, honk," cried the goose
with a splash and a waddle.
"The rain is so fun.
Hurry, don't dawdle."

"Bah to the rain," said the **goat** in a huff.
"I'd rather have sunshine
and play on the bluff."

"Meow,"
purred the cat.

"I don't care if it rains.
It's cozy on my rug,
where we sit and play games."

Whatever the weather

there are fun things to do.

We've seen the farm,

shall we go to the zoo?